9

8

FURRY TAILS

A bumper book of ten favourite animal tales

retold and illustrated by

Tony Ross

Andersen Press • London

Contents

MRS GOAT
AND HER SEVEN LITTLE KIDS

Once upon a time, Big Mother Goat was about to go to the supermarket.

"Kids," she said to her children, "don't you open that door to ANYONE. If you do, the hungry wolf will probably get in, and eat you all. Now we don't want that, do we?"

"No, we don't want that," said the kids.

"I'll kick him on the leg!" shouted the littlest one.

Now the Wolf was hiding underneath the window, and he heard all this. When Big Mother Goat had gone on her way, he knocked on the door.

"Who's that?" shouted the kids together.

"I'm your mum," the wolf growled. "Open up the door, I forgot to give you your pocket money."

"You're not Mum," shouted the littlest one. "Mum's got a squeaky little voice that sounds like music."

"You're the Hungry Wolf," shouted the kids, and they wouldn't open the door.

So the Wolf ran off to the music teacher's house.

"Teach me to speak in a squeaky little voice, like music," he growled. "If you don't, I'll bite your beak off."

"Very well," said the music teacher, and she did her best.

Then the wolf hurried back to the kids' house, and banged on the door. "Let me in, this is Mummy. I've got some sweets for you," he called.

"Show us your hoof first," said the littlest one, and the wolf pushed his paw through the letterbox.

"That's not Mum's hoof," cried the kids. "Mum's hoof's white. You're the Hungry Wolf."

The littlest one hit the paw with his little hammer, and the kids refused to open the door.

"OWWWWWWWCHHHH!" The wolf snatched his paw out of the letterbox, and sucked his fingers. "White, is it?" he snarled, and went off to find an artist.

"It's got to be white, with a little black bit at the end, just like a goat's hoof," he told the artist. "Make a good job of it, and I'll not bite your nose off."

The artist made a very good job of it, and the wolf hurried back to the house where the kids lived.

He banged on the door, and shouted in a squeaky little voice, like music, "Let me in, dearies. I've brought you some comics from the supermarket." The wolf waved his paw through the letterbox. "Look, it's Mummy."

"It's Mum's hoof all right," said one of the kids.

"And it's Mum's little squeaky voice, like music," said another. "Open the door."

"Not so fast . . ." said the littlest one. "Let's see your tail."

The wolf stuck his tail through the letterbox.

"Mum's tail is dainty, like an ear of wheat," said one kid. "This tail is grey and bushy, like . . . like . . ."

"Like the Hungry Wolf's tail," cried the littlest one. "Excuse me while I bite it."

The wolf howled, and the kids refused to open the door.

"So Mum's tail is dainty, like an ear of wheat, is it?" muttered the wolf, and he rushed off to see the dentist.

"I don't usually remove tails," said the dentist.

"If you don't remove this one, I'll bite your tail off," said the wolf.

"Then I'll make an exception in your case," said the dentist. "After all, I do have the necessary equipment. This'll not hurt."

The wolf stuck an ear of wheat where his tail had been, and once again banged on the kids' front door. "Let me in," he cried, in his little squeaky voice like music, waving his paw painted like a hoof. "I'm Mummy, and I've got ice cream."

He turned round, and wiggled his new tail.

"It's Mum's little voice, squeaky, like music," said one kid.

"It's Mum's hoof, white with a little black tip," said another.

"It's Mum's tail, dainty, like an ear of wheat," said a third.

"It's Mum!" they all shouted joyfully, and threw open the door. All that is, except the littlest one, who wasn't so sure, so he hopped into the coal bucket to hide.

In leaped the wolf, and swallowed six little kids whole.

"I thought there were seven," grumbled the wolf. "Seven would have been delicious. Still, six is okay."

So saying, he loosened his belt, and helped himself to a glass of Big Mother Goat's best beer.

The wolf took the beer into the back garden, and sat down in a wicker chair. Then, with an awful grin on his face, he dozed in the sun.

When Big Mother Goat got home, she was laden down with seven bags of sweets, seven comics, and seven ice creams.

The littlest one jumped out of the coal bucket, and told his mother exactly what had happened.

"He's still here, Mum," he bleated. "He's in the garden. He's in your chair."

"WHAT?" roared Big Mother Goat, dropping all her bags. "In my chair? With my kids in him? LET ME GET AT HIM!"

Big Mother Goat hit the dozing wolf at ninety miles an hour.

She butted him right out of the wicker chair.

She butted him so hard, that one of her kids shot out of his mouth.

She butted him again, and out came another.

"Not again!" pleaded the wolf, trying to crawl away. "Not on my bottom, my tail place still hurts . . . OW!"

She butted him again, and out flew a third kid.

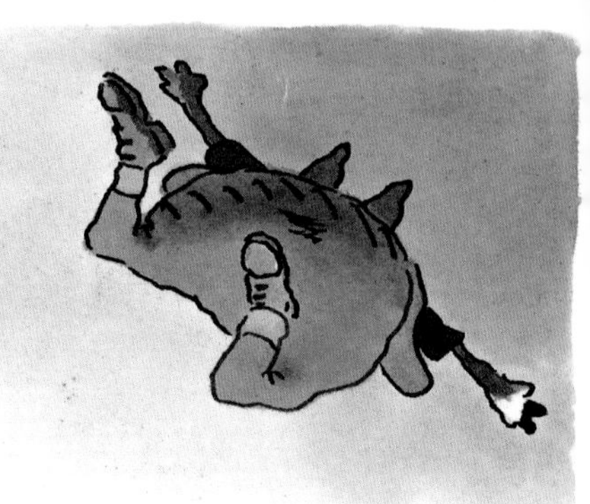

Altogether, Big Mother Goat butted the wolf seven times. Once each to get back her six swallowed children, and once to send the wolf right over the trees, and away for ever.

Then she gathered her kids around her, dried their tears, and gave each one a big kiss on the nose . . . and a slap on the ear for opening the door to a wolf.

STONE SOUP

One day, out walking, the Bad, Bad Wolf came across Mother Hen, pegging out her washing.

He studied the things hanging on the line, and he had to admit that they looked of the finest quality.

"Hmmm," thought the Wolf, " there are goodies to be had here."

So he stopped for a chat.

"Good day!" said the Wolf. "I think I shall eat you, and then steal all your goodies."

"Thank you very much," squawked Mother Hen. "But before that, perhaps you'd like some soup?"

"That's very kind of you," smiled the Bad, Bad Wolf. "I'd like some soup, *then* I'll eat you."

Mother Hen picked up a stone from the path.

"I'll make STONE SOUP," she said. "It's very special."

"It must be," said the Wolf. "I've eaten soup in all the best places, and I've never heard of it."

Mother Hen boiled some water, and dropped the stone into the pan.

As the Wolf didn't believe that soup could be made from a stone, he sipped a little from a spoon.

"*Peeeew!*" he spat. "It just tastes of hot water."

"Of *course* it does," snapped Mother Hen. "It just needs salt and pepper to bring out the flavour of the stone. While I'm doing that, why don't you just wash a few dishes?"

"Right!" laughed the Bad, Bad Wolf.

BoZ

When the Wolf had finished the dishes, he tasted the soup again.

"Yeeeuuugh!" he howled. "It's worse! It's like hot *salty* water now."

Maybe a couple of carrots will help the stone to cook," said Mother Hen. "While you're waiting, perhaps you could clean and dust the house?"

"Right!" grinned the Bad, Bad Wolf.

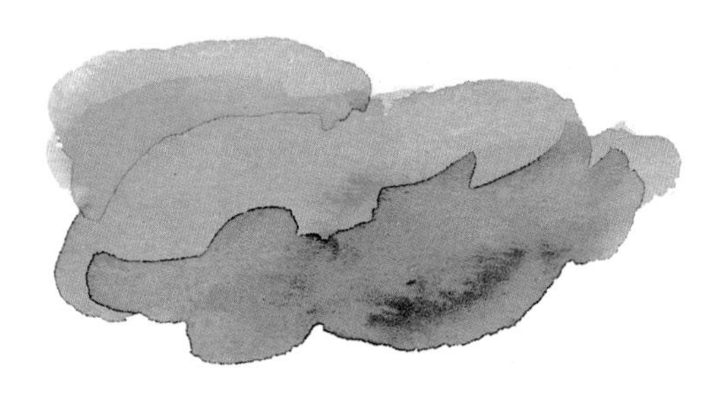

The Wolf tasted the stone soup again.

"It's not much better," he said.

"Potatoes!" cried Mother Hen. "Bless us, I did forget the potatoes." And she went to dig some up.

"While you're waiting," she called to the Wolf, "you *could* bring in the washing before it rains."

"Right," said the Bad, Bad Wolf.

Mother Hen let the Wolf taste the soup again.
"It's better," he said.
"But not quite right," fussed Mother Hen. "While I get some turnips, could you just cut that into a few logs?" As she handed him a tiny axe, she pointed to a huge tree. "And when you've finished, the stone soup should be just about ready."
"Right," muttered the Bad, Bad Wolf.

When the tree was cut into logs, the Wolf tasted the soup yet again.

"It's fine," he said. "Let's eat it *now*."

Mother Hen took a sip.

"Not yet," she said. "A sprout or two will really complement the flavour of the stone. While you're waiting, be a sweetie and fix the TV aerial on the roof."

"Right," groaned the Bad, Bad Wolf.

"The soup smells delicious!" panted the Wolf, when he came down off the roof.

"Ahhh," sniffed Mother Hen, "there's something missing . . . er . . . *mushrooms*, that's what it is, *mushrooms!*"

The Wolf stared.

"While you're waiting for the mushrooms to cook in," smiled Mother Hen, "you'd just have time to sweep the chimney."

"Right," snarled the Bad, Bad Wolf.

By the time the Wolf had finished the chimney, Mother Hen had thrown some beans, a little cabbage, a few lentils, and a marrow into the pan. Proudly she gave the Wolf a taste.

He was delighted.

"Who'd have thought," he sighed, "that a simple *stone* would make such a glorious soup!"

"I'm glad you liked it," said Mother Hen, when the Wolf had finished the soup. "You can eat me now."

"I *can't!*" gasped the Wolf. "I'm too full."

"Fancy that," said Mother Hen. "You'd better steal my goodies then, and be off with you."

The Bad, Bad Wolf leaped to his feet, and with a terrible roar . . .

. . . he snatched the stone, and took to his heels.

FOXY FABLES

THE FOX AND THE CROW

Madame Crow was very large and glossy black. When she was a small crowlet, someone told her that she had a lovely voice (for a crow), and ever since then she had fancied herself as an opera singer. She was an unbearable crow.

She would strut around town, feeling more important than everyone else, and close her eyes, throw her head back, and screech with her eyes shut. She couldn't see everyone running away with their hands over their ears. Madame Crow was a real pain.

One day Madame Crow was walking around the market when she spied a cheese stall. She stared at the wonderful cheeses on display: Cheddar, Mozzarella, blue ones, red ones, foreign ones . . . They looked yummy! "I-I-I-I-I thinnnnnnk I'll haaaaaave a piece of

Cheddar!" Madame Crow sang to a theme from "Madame Butterfly". And she just helped herself to a beakful.

"Hey, you!" shouted the stallkeeper. "Aren't you going to pay for that?"

"Let her have it," yelled all the other customers. "It'll keep her beak shut."

Madame Crow ignored everybody and hopped away with her piece of cheese. She went straight home and sat by the window, watching the world and hoping the world would watch her. She held the cheese firmly in her beak.

Just then a poor fox strolled by. He was very hungry. "That's a tasty piece of cheese," he thought as he stopped and looked up at Madame Crow.

"Gracious!" he gasped. "What a fine bird!"

Madame Crow glanced down and smiled mysteriously.

"Such obvious breeding, such beauty!"

Madame Crow wriggled with delight.

"Those flashing eyes, those slender, blue-black quills . . ."

Madame Crow peered down at the fox, waiting for more compliments. Then she frowned.

"Perhaps he is unaware of my exceptionally fine voice," she thought. Madame Crow leaned out of her window and tried to impress the fox with a couple of verses of "Come into the garden, Maud".

As she opened her beak to sing, the cheese fell out . . . down to the street below.

The fox grabbed the cheese and gobbled it up. "Exquisite!" he said, and went on his way.

THE CAT AND THE FOX

One day the fox was walking in the park when he met the most beautiful cat he had ever seen. She was smaller than the fox, but not very much. Her nose was shorter, but not very much. Her tail was thinner, but not very much. All in all she looked enough like the fox for him to fall in love with her.

The cat, however, didn't think much of the fox. She thought that he was a show-off, and anyway, she didn't like redheads. Soon the fox found out where the cat lived, and he hung around every day hoping to see her. Whenever she stepped out of her front door, the fox would spring forward, take her paw, and walk with her. The cat was much too polite to tell the fox to get lost; after all she had a pedigree.

The fox liked to talk about himself all the time. "I've got a boat on the river!" he said.

"Indeed?" smiled the cat. "I hate water!"

"I drink whisky with no ice!" smirked the fox. "Would you like some?"

"Gracious no!" said the cat, smiling. "I prefer milk."

"I know a thousand and one tricks," giggled the fox. "How many do you know?"

The cat struggled to remember her manners and not use rude words with this silly, bushy-tailed nitwit. "How clever!" she yawned. "I only know *one*."

Their walk had taken the two animals into the rough part of town, and they ran into a gang of wolves and bad dogs, all stretched out across the pavement. The cat shot up the nearest tree.

The fox tried his thousand and one tricks. He tried judo and karate, but the gang just punched his nose. He tried telling jokes, but the gang didn't understand them and boxed his ears. He tried to argue, but the gang wouldn't listen. It was more fun to kick the fox up into the air. Silliest of all, he tried to fight back and bit a bad dog's tail. Enraged, the bad dog swung the fox into the air and slammed him against the pavement. Then, tiring of their game, the nasty gang left.

The badly battered fox looked up into the tree where the cat sat safely. "So what's your one trick?" he snarled.

"I can climb trees," she purred.

THE FOX AND THE GOAT

One hot day there were some *terrible* smells drifting around the Foxes' house. Mr Fox didn't mind too much, but Mrs Fox did. She looked all over to find the cause of the awful smells. Mr Fox watched TV. At last the trouble was found – the drains were blocked.

Mrs Fox said to her husband, "Unless you do something about those drains, I will call the plumber and that will cost you a lot of money."

"I'll do it right away," said Mr Fox. He put on his jeans, found his brush and torch, and went into the street. He pulled up the manhole

cover and hopped into the opening, landing with a splash in two feet of dirty water. The smell was even worse down there.

Mr Fox tried to clear the drain, but he couldn't – he'd left his brush on the street. "I'll have to go and get my tools!" he muttered angrily, and then, to his horror he found that he couldn't climb out of the drain. The walls were too steep and slippery. The silly fox hadn't thought of bringing a ladder, so he sat in the smelly water, slapping himself on the nose, and telling himself what an idiot he'd been.

Suddenly a voice came from above. "Hello!"

Mr Fox looked up. It was the crazy old goat from across the street.

"What are you doing down there?" asked the goat.

"Relaxing in the water," said Mr Fox. "You know, health-giving springs."

"Doesn't smell too healthy," said the goat, who wasn't *that* crazy.
"No," agreed Mr Fox, "but then, things that are good for you are often pretty nasty, aren't they?"

The goat thought about all the medicine he'd ever taken and about all the food he didn't like that was supposed to be good for him.

"Yes," he said. "Mind if I come down and share your cure?"

"Be my guest," grinned Mr Fox. "There's enough smelly water for both of us."

So the crazy goat jumped down into the drain too. As soon as he did, Mr Fox used his horns as a ladder and scrambled up onto the street.

"I don't like it here," cried the goat. "How do I get out?"

"I'll go and get a ladder," grinned Mr Fox and he threw his brush down. "It'll take some time, so while I'm gone, you might as well clear that drain!"

THE FOX AND THE STORK

The Fox loved to eat out, but since it was so expensive, nobody would go with him. And the fox *hated* to eat alone.

One evening outside the theatre he ran into his friend the stork, who was an actor and a very funny fellow. "How about dinner in a nice café?" said the fox, trotting after him.

"Oh, dear, no," said the stork. "I can't afford the kind of place you like to go to."

"Please come," pleaded the fox. "I really love to hear your stories and I'll pay."

"Very well," sighed the stork. He did feel very hungry.

When the two friends arrived at the café, the stork was ravenous. The head waiter handed the menu to the fox. "I'll order for us both. Asparagus soup, please, for my friend and me."

The soup was served in shallow soup dishes, and while the fox was able to lap his up with relish, the stork couldn't because his long, thin beak was useless with the wide, shallow dish. "Not hungry?" sniggered the fox. "Don't worry, I'll find room for yours." And so the crafty fox ate *both* bowls of soup at no extra cost.

The stork sat back and looked around. "A nice place," he said, "but I know a better one. Do you want to go there for pudding?"

"Why not?" smiled the fox. "Why not top a splendid soup with a splendid pudding?"

The head waiter at the next café seemed to know the stork. "Good evening, Sir," he said. "A table for two?"

"Near the door," said the stork. They sat down and the stork took the menu before the fox could get his paws on it. "Two knickerbocker glories," he ordered.

When they arrived they were ice cream with fruit, served in the tallest, thinnest glasses the fox had ever seen. The fox could only get his snout into the very top of the glass, but the stork could sink his long beak right down to the bottom. After finishing every drop, the stork looked at the fox who was still struggling to get his fat nose into the long thin glass. "Not hungry?" The stork smiled, and taking the knickerbocker glory from the fox he gobbled it all down.

The waiter came by. "Is everything all right?" he asked.

"Yes, thank you," said the stork. "My friend is paying." And with that, he slipped quickly out of the door.

THE STAG AND HIS MIRRORS

A stag had just moved into a flat in town. He went into a big store and bought some chairs, a TV, and a video recorder. Still the flat needed something. Ah, that was it! The walls were bare!

The stag ran back to the store and asked to see some paintings. The salesman showed him lots – all with stags standing on hills. "Don't you have anything more . . . well . . . cheerful?" said the stag.

"No more paintings," said the salesman, "but you are such a handsome chap, have you considered a mirror?"

"Handsome chap. Hmmm," thought the stag. "I'll take one!" he said.

The salesman didn't think the stag was particularly handsome, but at least he'd sold a mirror.

The stag hung his mirror over the fireplace. "I certainly am

handsome," he said. "Look at the graceful curve of those horns!"

The stag admired his horns every day, and as time went by he hung mirrors on all his walls so he could see his handsome horns wherever he looked.

"Now I must buy a *big* mirror to stand on the floor," thought the vain animal so he hurried back to the department store.

The salesman showed him a beautiful long mirror, and the stag stepped back to admire himself. What a shock he got! In the smaller mirrors he had only seen his head and shoulders. Now he could see all of himself . . . those wonderful horns . . . and . . . oh, dear . . . those silly, spindly, thin, funny-looking, hairy, awful little legs.

The stag refused to buy the mirror and rushed out of the store.

Outside he ran . . . bump . . . into a gang of uncouth wolves back from a football match. "Get him!" they screamed, pointing at the stag.

The stag ran off and his silly, spindly, thin, funny-looking, hairy, awful little legs allowed him to escape from the wolves. He ran much faster than any of them . . . but he wasn't looking where he was going and he tangled his handsome horns in the overhead trolley bus wires . . .

and a trolley bus was coming.

THE HARE AND THE TORTOISE

One night the Hare was having a quiet drink with the Tortoise, and as usual the conversation turned to sport. Also as usual the Hare was bragging about how good he was at cricket, snooker, darts . . . everything. As he spoke he kept poking the Tortoise on the shell. At last the Tortoise snapped, "You may be okay at all the *easy* sports, but I'm a better *athlete* than you."

Suddenly the bar went quiet. The Tortoise wished he'd kept his big mouth shut. The Hare couldn't believe his long ears. "Running, you mean?" he said.

"Running!" gulped the Tortoise. "You may well be a fine bowler of the googly, but I'm the better runner." And so a race was arranged for the next day. The Tortoise went home to bed wondering why he ever said such ridiculous things.

The following day a 1500-metre course was marked out by the Mole who owned a starting pistol. The Hare and the Tortoise took off their tracksuits and went to the starting line. The Mole pointed his pistol into the air and pulled the trigger. The Hare shot off as if he'd been stung. As he went around the first bend, the Tortoise was still trying to get his feet out of the starting blocks.

After the first thousand metres the Hare stopped and looked back. He couldn't even see the Tortoise. "This is no fun," he muttered. "I want the Tortoise to *see* me win. I'll wait here while he catches up."Having decided this, the Hare sat under a tree and fell asleep in the sun.

Twenty minutes later the Tortoise came plodding along, wheezing badly. The Hare sat up and waved as the Tortoise creaked past. "Time to go!" laughed the Hare, and he leaped up. What he didn't notice was the low branch just above his head, and he crashed his silly head into it, and knocked himself out.

The Tortoise plodded on towards the finishing line. When the Hare regained his senses, he hurried towards the finish, but it was too late. The Tortoise had already crossed the line, was wearing the gold-plated medal, and was doing press-ups.

As the hot and angry Hare crossed the line to the jeers of the crowd, the Tortoise looked up.

"What are you like at highjumping?" he grinned.

BIG, BAD BARNEY BEAR

Moose was bored, so he decided to go and find a job.

He found lots of work on the building site.

One shovel looked better than the others . . .

. . . so Moose chose it for himself.

Moose was not happy, but he started work.

He worked hard for an hour, until it was time for coffee.

Moose chose the cup that would hold the most coffee, but he had to take a smaller one.

Moose was not happy. He took his small cup of coffee and settled in a large comfy chair . . .

. . . but he had to move onto an uncomfortable pile of bricks.

Moose was not happy, he could take no more . . .

. . . and the other animals trembled.

The crocodile pointed to a factory that
BIG, BAD BARNEY BEAR had built . . .

. . . but Moose was not impressed.
He wanted to find the bear . . .

. . . and put him in his place . . .

. . . once and for all!

At daybreak, Moose came across a lonely cottage, big enough for a bear.

He knocked on the door, and it was opened by a huge animal.

With a roar, Moose charged. Skin and teeth flew, fur and trouser buttons . . .

. . . until at last, Moose was the winner.

The bear was bruised, and baffled . . .

and didn't seem to understand . . .

. . . why.

THE BOY WHO CRIED WOLF!

Once upon a time a little boy lived on this side of the mountains. His name was Harry.

On the other side of the mountains a wolf lived in the lap of luxury. Nobody ever asked *his* name.

The wolf had fine manners (for a wolf).
Sometimes he put on his dinner jacket . . .

and came over the mountains
. . . for dinner.

Because the wolf liked dining on people, everybody on this side of the mountains was afraid of him. So . . .

whenever Harry had to do something he hated, like having a bath,

he would cry, "Wolf!" (even if the wolf was nowhere to be seen).
Because everybody was afraid of the wolf . . .

Harry was left alone to do just what he wanted.

Once a week Harry went for his violin lesson. Because he hated lessons . . .

he cried, "Wolf!" even though the wolf was not around.

Then Harry was left alone to play the kind of music *he* liked.

Sometimes Harry even cried, "Wolf!"
just for the fun of it.

One day Harry was cycling in the mountains
when the wolf jumped out of the rocks.

"WOLF!" cried Harry.
He ran back to the town crying, "WOLF! WOLF!"
all the way.

"WOLF!" cried Harry, but his grandmother didn't believe him. Harry always cried, "Wolf!"
"Tell me another one," she said.

"WOLF!" cried Harry, but nobody listened.

"Save me from the WOLF!" shrieked Harry,
but everybody laughed.
"Harry's crying 'wolf' again," they said.

At last the wolf caught up with Harry.
"You shouldn't have told so many lies!"
said the grown-ups sternly.

The wolf heard the grown-ups and changed his mind about eating Harry.

He ate the grown-ups instead.

Then . . .

he changed his mind again and had Harry for supper.

C'est la vie.

First published in Great Britain in 1999 by Andersen Press Ltd., 20 Vauxhall Bridge Road,
London SW1V 2SA. Published in Australia by Random House Australia Pty.,
20 Alfred Street, Milsons Point, Sydney, NSW 2061.
Colour separated in Switzerland by Photolitho AG, Zürich.
Printed and bound in Italy by Grafiche AZ, Verona.

10 9 8 7 6 5 4 3 2 1

British Library Cataloguing in Publication Data available.
ISBN 0 86264 926 9
This book has been printed on acid-free paper